DATE DUE

2-10-86	DEC 2 1992	AUG 1 4 2013	
3-12	SEP 2 1 1993		
5-1-86	DEC 8 1993		
1-1-87	FEB 9 1994		
MAR 10 89	MAY 17 1995		
5-28-89	NOV 1 0 1998		
7-30-89	MAR 1 0 1999		
10-14-89	MAR 3 1 1999		
11-19-89	DEC 2 9 1999		
12-14-89	MAY 1 8 2001		
5-19	FEB 0 7 2011		
9-25-90			
2-14-91			
4-6-91			
5-25-91			
NOV 2 2 1991			
FEB 7 1992			
APR 2 1 1995			

GAYLORD   PRINTED IN U.S.A.

GRANPA

John Burningham

CROWN PUBLISHERS, INC. • NEW YORK

Published in the United States in 1985 by Crown Publishers, Inc., One Park Avenue, New York, New York 10016

Originally published in Great Britain by Jonathan Cape Limited, 30 Bedford Square, London WC1

Manufactured in Italy

Library of Congress Cataloging in Publication Data
Burningham, John.
Granpa.

Summary: A little girl and her grandfather share very special moments.
1. Children's stories, English. [1. Grandfathers – Fiction]   I. Title.
PZ7.B936Gr   1984   [E]   84-17464

ISBN: 0-517-55643-X
10 9 8 7 6 5 4 3 2 1

First American Edition

And how's my little girl?

There will not be room for all the little seeds to grow

Do worms go to Heaven?

Row row row your boat
gently down the stream

*Little ducks, soup and sheep, sunshine in
the trees…*

I didn't know Teddy was another
little girl.

Noah knew that the ark was not far from land when he saw the dove carrying the olive branch.

Could we float away in this house, Granpa?

That was not a nice thing

to say to Granpa.

This is lovely chocolate ice-cream.

It's not chocolate. It's strawberry!

When we get to the beach can we stay there for ever?

Yes, but we must go back for our tea at four o'clock.

When I've finished this lollipop can we get some more? I need the sticks to make things.

When I was a boy we used to roll our
wooden hoops down the street
after school.

Were you once a baby as well, Granpa?

If I catch a fish we can cook it for supper.

What if you catch a whale, Granpa?

Harry, Florence and I used to come
down that hill like little arrows.
I remember one Christmas…

You nearly slipped then, Granpa.

Granpa can't come out to play today.

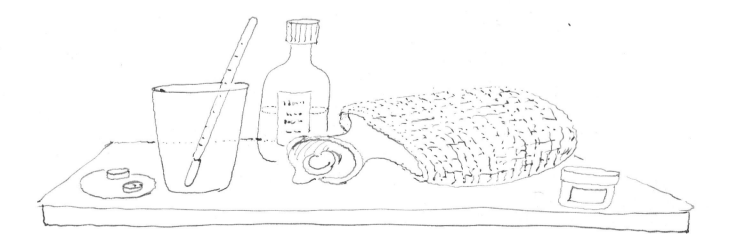

Tomorrow shall we go to Africa, and you can be the captain?